Squishy McFluff
The Invisible Cat

On with the Show!

About Pip Jones

Pip lives in Clevedon with her partner, her two daughters and a real invisible cat. Pip won the Greenhouse Funny Prize in 2012 with *Squishy McFluff: The Invisible Cat*. She is the author of six other Squishy McFluff books, several picture books (including *Daddy's Sandwich*, *Izzy Gizmo* and *The Chocolate Monster*) and her chapter book series, Piggy Handsome.

About Ella Okstad

Ella returned to her native Norway after graduating where she now illustrates children's books. When she is not at her desk, she is at home with her husband, three boys and a cat. Squishy is her first imaginary cat. She has also illustrated *Ballerina Dreams*, *Tiny Tantrum* and *Sophie Johnson: Unicorn Expert*.

FABER & FABER

has published children's books since 1929. Some of our very first publications included Old Possum's Book of Practical Cats by T. S. Eliot starring the now world-famous Macavity, and *The Iron Man* by Ted Hughes. Our catalogue at the time said that 'it is by reading such books that children learn the difference between the shoddy and the genuine'. We still believe in the power of reading to transform children's lives.

Squishy McFluff
The Invisible Cat

On with the Show!

by *Pip Jones*

Illustrated by *Ella Okstad*

FABER & FABER

First published in 2020
by Faber and Faber Limited
Bloomsbury House
74–77 Great Russell Street
London WC1B 3DA

Designed by Faber and Faber
Printed in India

A CIP record for this book is available from the British Library

978–0–571–35036–0

MIX
Paper from
responsible sources
FSC® C016779
FSC
www.fsc.org

2 4 6 8 10 9 7 5 3 1

For you, Mum, with love always. xxxx

Can you see him? My kitten?

Look, he's acting the clown!

We're excited because

there's a circus in town!

Imagine him, quick!

Have you imagined enough?

Oh good! You can see him!

It's Squishy McFluff!

One balmy evening,

on a Friday in May,

As Mummy was putting

the sandpit away,

She sighed a long sigh,

then said: 'Everyone!

'I've a plan for the morning.

It'll be SO much fun!

'Oh, just WAIT 'til I tell you . . . !'

(Dad groaned with dread.)

'Tomorrow, we're all going to . . .

TIDY THE SHED!'

'What?! Noooooooooooo!!'

Ava hugged her invisible cat.

'Squishy McFluff says

he won't enjoy THAT!

'Just look at his face.

Aw, you've made him feel sad!

'His whiskers are drooping!'

Mum said: 'Too bad!

'It's time for pyjamas.'

Ava let out a yawn . . .

Then the breeze blew

Dad's newspaper over the lawn.

McFluff (silently) miaowed!

Ava gasped in delight!

On the cover, the words read:

This Saturday night!
Bing's Big Top Circus
is coming to town!
Starring

HANK HONK

the world's craziest clown!

'Mum! Dad! Quick, LOOK!'

Ava showed them the pages.

CIRCUS

HANK
HONK

TONIGHT'S
MAIN EVENT

'I've wanted to go to

a circus for AGES!

'Oh pleaaaase can we go!'

Ava begged on her knees.

'Squish has never seen clowns!

Or a swinging trapeze!

'Or a fancy-pants lady

who breathes out real fire!

'Or a man doing cartwheels,

high up on a wire,

or . . .'

'Shhh!'

Mum took the paper.

She looked apprehensive.

'Oh, Ava! These tickets

'Are very expensive . . .'

'The deal is,' said Mum,

'if you don't make a fuss,

'If you help out tomorrow,

and you tidy with us,

'Then I will buy the tickets,

'cos once that shed's done,

'We'll really deserve to go out

and have fun!'

Early next morning

they were up and about

In time to catch Dad

as he tried to sneak out!

'And where are
YOU off to?'

'Er, the lake . . . ?' Dad replied.

'Not likely!' said Mum.

So they all tramped outside.

The shed door was opened.

Out the junk clattered:

The sandpit, some buckets,

a tent which was tattered,

Then plant pots and paint pots

and badminton rackets,

Some rusty old shelves with their

rusty old brackets.

And then, last of all, with

an almighty rumble,

A mountain of toys

toppled down in

a jumble.

Mum began sorting . . .

but McFluff had a plan.

He swung on the spout of the

watering can!

'I think you're right, Squish!

As a matter of fact,

There's lots of stuff here

we could use for our act!

'We'll find things to balance,

and find things to throw.

'We need practice to join

a big circus, you know!'

They made wooden stilts.

Ava clung to the wall.

'We just can't walk straight when

we're terribly tall!'

19

They found an old bike and

removed the front wheel.

'We can't join the circus on THIS!'

Ava squealed.

They got lots of pots, but soon

Ava was struggling.

'I'm not sure that these are the right

shape for juggling!'

20

They tackled the tightrope!

It was ever so high.

'Mum, please can you help . . . ?!'

Ava said with a sigh.

Plucking her down, Mum said:

'Listen. Tonight,

'We're WATCHING the circus . . .

NOT performing, alright?

'You said you'd both help!

If you DO want to go,

'The shed is just there . . . so now,

ON WITH THE SHOW!'

By six-thirty that evening,

Ava was ready

(Complete with a headdress,

all rather unsteady).

So the family set off,

with twinkling smiles,

To drive to the circus.

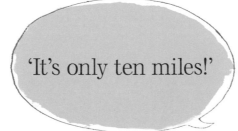

'It's only ten miles!'

They whizzed through the sunshine,

and hadn't gone far

When Squish saw a chap

standing next to a car.

The man poked the engine,

then gave it a CLOUT . . .

Which made a huge puff

of black smoke billow out!

'Not now!' the man wailed.

'This can't happen TODAY!'

'Oh, crumpets!' said Ava.

'Do we think he's okay?'

Squish pointed. 'Ah, YES!'

Ava said. 'Now I see.

'He's smiling! He looks

pretty happy to me.'

27

The traffic lights changed,

    and so off the car sped.

They drove and they drove till . . .

    'Look, THERE!' Up ahead,

All stripes and bright lights,

    the Big Top loomed high,

With its colourful flag

    swaying high in the sky.

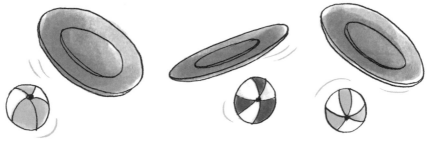

'Wow!' Ava whispered

    as they walked through the gates,

And passed a performer

    who was spinning twelve plates!

Then a strong man! A juggler!

    The band played so loud,

As dancers did backflips

    to welcome the crowd.

There was still half an hour

before the show's start.

'I'm famished!' said Dad

when he spotted a cart

Selling popcorn and candies

and ice creams and sweets.

'I'll get us some snacks,

then we'll all take our seats.'

Ava and Squish both

skipped off to the tent,

Where a poster read:

HANK HONK

TONIGHT'S MAIN EVENT

While Dad watched his popcorn

    get oozily buttered,

They peeped through the gap . . .

    'Huh, you what?' someone muttered.

The Ring Master, Bing,

    was right there, on his phone.

'Please tell me you're joking!'

    he said with a groan,

As a big bead of sweat

trickled over his brow.

'But you're our finale!

Just get here RIGHT NOW!

'You can't? HANK, I TOLD YOU

TO GET A NEW CAR!

'Well, find me a new act!

This show NEEDS A STAR!'

'Oh, dear,' Ava sighed.

Mum said: 'Hey! Why so glum?'

'Squishy's sad. It's Hank Honk!

I don't think he can come!'

'Don't worry,' said Mum.

She squeezed Ava's shoulder.

'You'll learn lots tonight!

For when you're MUCH older.'

Ava looked puzzled.

'For the circus!' Mum smiled.

'And when you both join, oh,

the crowds will go wild . . . !'

Well, that cheered them both up!

Ava squealed, 'Yaaaay!'

She just wished SO much

they could join right away.

'INTRODUCING . . .' she sang

(as she tipped her tall hat).

'AWESOME AVA! AAAAAAND

HER INVISIBLE CAT!'

Baby Roo giggled,

and Mum and Dad laughed.

'Such rascals!' said Daddy.

'You two are so daft!'

Then suddenly Bing,

the Ring Master, appeared.

'Ahem!' he said, twirling

the end of his beard.

38

'Excuse me, but, erm . . .

did I hear you quite right?

'That you are our substitute

act for tonight . . . ?

'You got here so quickly!'

'No, no . . .' Mum began,

But instantly Squishy McFluff

had a plan!

Ava beamed. Squish stood tall.

'We are indeed, YES!

'Oh, we're such a great act!

You NEVER will guess

'All the tricks an invisible cat

can perform . . . !'

'Remarkable!' Bing said.

'You'll go down a storm!

'I've never **heard** of

    an act this tremendous!

'An invisible cat!

    Yes, YES! It's stupendous!

'We need costumes!

    One see-through! One extra small!

'We'll have you both ready

    in no time at all!'

Ava, all dressed up

in sequins and spangles,

With sparkling beads

and jingling bangles,

Scooped up McFluff and then

peered at the ring.

'You can take a look round

if you want to,' called Bing.

They hopped, skipped and jumped

to a giant trampoline –

The tallest and widest

that they'd EVER seen!

But when they climbed on, well . . .

the bounce wasn't right.

'Oh bother! I think it's

because we're too light!'

Ava said, 'Hmmmm . . .'

Then McFluff had a thought!

'Good idea! If we make

this elastic more taut,

'It's bound to get SO much more

boing-y and springy!

'I'll just turn this wotsit, and

pull on this thingy . . .'

But then (just as soon as they'd

stretched the elastic)

Out rang a voice:

'Are we ready? Fantastic!

'Let's open the doors!

We should let the crowd in!'

'Oops! Quick, Squish!

The show is about to begin!'

'Ladie-eeeeees and gentlemennnnn!

    Boyyyyyyys and girrrrrrls . . . !'

The dancers took off

    doing fast twists and twirls.

Seven ladies took turns

    to breathe out real fire!

And four men did cartwheels

high up on the wire!

Jugglers! And tumblers!

They were so acrobatic.

Ava clapped wildly –

she was truly ecstatic!

Until . . . Bing returned

    to the beat of a drum,

And Ava knew then

    that their moment had come!

'In a change to our scheduled

    programme tonight,

'I proudly present,

    for your joy and delight . . . '

(In the glare of the bulbs,

Ava tipped her tall hat.)

'AMAZING AVA! AAAAAAND . . .

HER INVISIBLE CAT!'

The crowd went bananas!

They began to applaud

And stomp their feet madly!

'HOORAY!' someone roared.

Then . . . all . . . went . . . quiet . . .

Hush swept through the crowd.

The silence seemed

suddenly deafeningly loud!

Ava gulped in the spotlight.

Bing gave her a prod.

From the sidelines

Mum gave an encouraging nod.

Ava breathed deeeeeply,

then held out her hand.

McFluff jumped right on it . . .

and did a headstand!

'Behold! The incredible

Squishy McFluff!

'He does cartwheels! And backflips!

And all sorts of stuff!

'Just LOOK AT HIM GO!'

Ava beamed with pure glee . . .

But soon there were murmurs of:

'Huh?' 'I can't see . . .'

56

'But where . . . ?' 'What's it doing?'

'This act is a swizz!'

'We can't watch his tricks,

we don't know where he is!'

Bing loosened his collar,

and then bent down low:

'Where IS he? Do something!

Quick! On with the show!'

Well McFluff, so excited,

decided to play!

And the audience gasped

when they heard Ava say:

'Behind you, behind you!

Mind where you stand!

'He's right by your shoe!

Now he's sniffing your hand!

'He's jumped on your shoulder!

His tail's in your EAR!

'Look harder! Turn quicker!

No, not THERE . . .

he's here!'

The people were no longer

    mumbling and jeering.

They got to their feet –

    they were laughing and cheering!

'I think I can see him!'

    'That cat's SUPER quick!'

'Watch him closely!' 'Oh, YES!'

'An **incredible** trick!'

Bing yelled: 'I can't see him!

What?! This is absurd!'

And THEN . . .

something really amazing occurred.

Still hopping about the place,

suddenly Bing

Bashed into the huge trampoline

and then . . . PING!

Squish grabbed the elastic.

He was flung very high!

'You SEE?' Ava pointed.

'LOOK! Squishy can FLY!'

So all of the audience

followed her gaze,

And said, 'Oh, my gosh!' –

they were truly amazed

To watch the trapeze

as it swung loop the loops,

Propelling McFluff through

six pendulum hoops,

Then on to the bike,

which then started to roll . . .

Squish ran to the end

of the balancing pole

Just as it teetered,

 and then tipped, and then fell!

Of course, Squishy plummeted

 quickly as well

. . . Right into the CANON!

And one . . . two . . . three . . . BOOM!

Over the crowd, like a rocket,

he ZOOOOOOOOMED!

The fireworks went off

as he dropped on the mat.

'Hooray!' Ava shouted.

'That's Squishy, my cat!'

'SQUI-SHY! SQUI-SHY!'

came the chants from the crowd.

McFluff ran to Ava.

They hugged . . . then they bowed.

Mum cried, 'Gosh, you're REALLY

the stars of the show!'

'So we CAN join the circus, then . . . ?'

Mummy said . . .

'No!'